SOUND POEMS

MORE Interactive Listening and Reading Fun
By Cristi Cary Miller

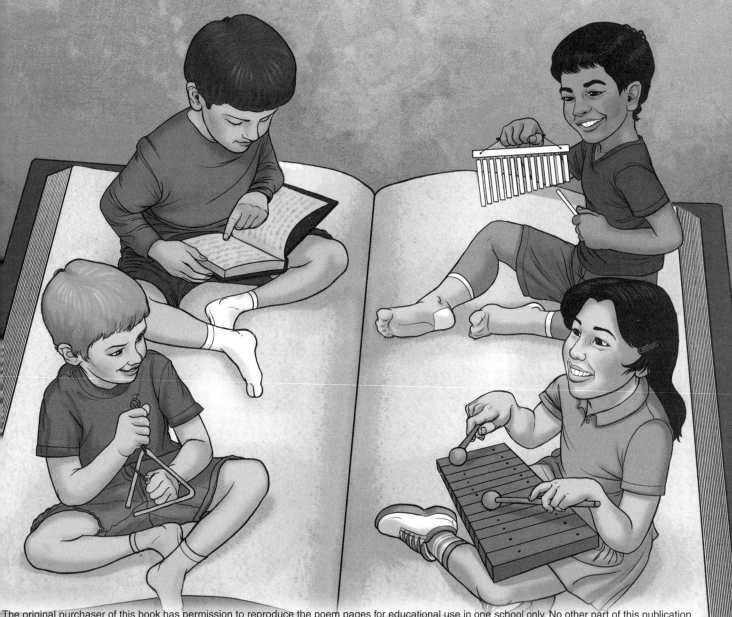

The original purchaser of this book has permission to reproduce the poem pages for educational use in one school only. No other part of this publication may be reproduced in any form or by any means without the prior written permission of the Publisher. Any other use is strictly prohibited.

HAL•LEONARD® CORPORATION

7777 W. BLUEMOUND RD. P.O. BOX 13819 MILWAUKEE, WI 53213

Copyright © 2013 by HAL LEONARD CORPORATION
International Copyright Secured   All Rights Reserved

Visit Hal Leonard Online at
www.halleonard.com

TABLE OF CONTENTS

HOW TO USE CD-ROM

Adobe Reader 9: This interactive PDF must be opened with Adobe Reader 9 or later. If you do not currently have this, we have included the program on this disc for you. Once Adobe Reader 9 is installed, follow the PDF access instructions below.

PDF Access:

1. **INSERT** the "Sound Poems" disc into your computer and **OPEN**.
   For PC Users: Go to "My Computer," then right-click on the disc drive or the "Sound Poems" disc icon. Click "Open" or "Explore."
   For Mac Users: Double-click on the "Sound Poems" disc icon.

2. **DVD Contents:**
   • Adobe Reader 9 folder with applications for Mac and PC
   • "Read Me First" PDF file of these instructions
   • "Sound Poems" icon folder

3. **COPY** this "Sound Poems" folder to the desktop of your computer. This file transfer may take a few minutes.
   For PC Users: Right-click/select "copy"; then go to desktop and right-click/paste.
   For Mac Users: Drag the folder icon onto the desktop.

4. **OPEN** the folder by double-clicking the "Sound Poems" folder icon you have just copied to your desktop. You will see the "Sound Poems" PDF and a folder of Resources.

5. **Double-click the "Sound Poems" PDF file to begin!**

Main Menu:
From the Main Menu, simply click on a poem title to access a projectable color version of that poem. From the poem screen, you can access black/white PDFs of the selected poem and rhythm sound effects from 2 icons (upper left). To return to Main Menu, click the pink "home" icon (bottom right). To close the program, click "Close" icon (bottom right) on Main Menu screen.

Learning to read is one of the most exciting and important parts of a child's life. Through literature, children lose themselves inside their heads as they discover the world of imagination. A follow-up to the popular "Sound Stories," "Sound Poems" offers more cross-curricular fun by incorporating music into classic poetry, famous speeches and documents of history like never before!

These 18 reproducible poems contain highlighted words that, when read, indicate special instrumental sounds and rhythmic motifs are to be played by your students. If you don't have all the instruments suggested, substitute or consider body percussion. There are many choices to create your presentation. The teaching suggestions provide a framework for instruction, but can be manipulated to best fit your students' abilities. The enclosed CD-ROM offers projectable and printable options. You can read the poem or select several of your students to read. And don't forget about the possibility of acting out these poems. It will only make the experience richer for your students as well as add a lot of enjoyment. Doesn't this "sound" like fun? You bet!

National Standards for Arts Education in Music

The following objectives are met through this resource:

#2 Performing on instruments, alone and with others, a varied repertoire of music

#5 Reading and notating music

#8 Understanding relationships between music, the other arts, and disciplines outside the arts

Cristi Miller is highly regarded across the United States as a master teacher, conductor and composer. After graduating from Oklahoma State University, she began her teaching career instructing grades 7-12. She eventually moved to the Putnam City School system in 1989 where she worked in the elementary classroom for 21 years. In 1992, Mrs. Miller was selected as the Putnam City Teacher of the Year and in 1998 received one of the four "Excellence in Education" awards given through the Putnam City Foundation. In 2008, she became a National Board Certified Teacher and in 2009, she was selected as the Putnam City PTA Teacher of the Year. Recently, Mrs. Miller became a part of the Fine Arts Staff at Heritage Hall Schools in the Oklahoma City area where she teaches middle school music. Cristi has served as the Elementary Representative on the Oklahoma Choral Directors Association Board of Directors as well as the Elementary Vice President for the Oklahoma Music Educators Association. She currently serves as the President for this organization. Along with her teaching responsibilities, Cristi authors and co-authors a column for a national music magazine entitled Music Express and was a contributing writer for the Macmillan McGraw-Hill music textbook series, Spotlight on Music. In addition, she serves as the consulting editor for Little Schoolhouse book series, "Christopher Kazoo and Bongo Boo." Mrs. Miller is frequently in demand as a clinician and director across the United States and Canada with numerous choral pieces and books in publication through Hal Leonard Corporation. She has also been the recipient of several ASCAP awards for her music. Cristi and her husband, Rick, live in Oklahoma City.

DADDY FELL INTO THE POND

Welcome to the world of Sound Poems! These activities are designed to reinforce your students' reading and listening skills and, at the same time, add some music fun. Each poem contains "special words" that are attached to sounds and rhythms. These instrumental inserts will enhance the poem as your students become the "sound effects." Use the suggested instruments or substitute with those that are available. There are many choices for presentation. You can read the poem and have your students play their patterns/ sounds, or select several of them to read. And don't forget about the possibility of acting out these poems. It will only make the experience richer for your students as well as add a lot of enjoyment.

Our first poem comes from the poet, Alfred Noyes. This writer was born in 1880 in Wolverhampton, England. Although best known for his ballad, "The Highwayman," this selected poem is sure to bring a smile to your students' faces as they envision what Noyes brings to life through his work.

TEACHING SUGGESTIONS

1. Project the poem (found on CD-ROM) or hand out printed copies. Then read the poem aloud for the students as they follow along, alternately patting a dotted quarter note beat. Emphasize a 6/8 meter as you recite the verses. (Because Noyes wrote the words "Then" and "When" on separate lines, this might indicate that these words are held out longer. For this presentation, hold these words out for 2 beats.)

2. Repeat the above step as the children speak the poem with you.

3. Finally, have the students read the poem aloud as they clap on the highlighted words. (To secure the feel for this meter even further, have students practice one more time reading the poem internally, but continuing to clap on the highlighted words.)

4. Focus on the rhythmic motif, "Daddy fell into the pond." Clap the pattern for the students while speaking the motif words. Have students echo speak the pattern. Transfer to instrument.

5. Explain the tremolo for "Then/When" and have students practice on their legs. Transfer to instrument.

6. Point out the similarities between the motifs "merry and bright" and "Timothy danced." Have students echo speak/clap the pattern with motif words then transfer to instruments.

7. Repeat the above step for the motifs "quick, oh quick" and "silently." Transfer to instruments.

8. Discuss the laughed motif and what the line connected to the sound tells the performer to do. Transfer to instrument.

9. Speak/clap the remaining motifs and transfer to instruments.

10. Choose a reader(s) to recite the poem as the instrumentalists play on their selected words.

11. For fun, try reciting the poem internally with the instruments playing on highlighted words.

DADDY FELL INTO THE POND

GRUMBLED
guiro

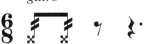

GRAY
cowbell

SAY
woodblock

DAY
hand drum

THEN/WHEN
bass xylophone (or keyboard)

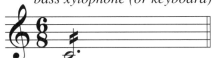

DADDY FELL INTO THE POND
conga drum

FACE
finger cymbals

MERRY AND BRIGHT
maracas

TIMOTHY DANCED
temple blocks

QUICK, OH QUICK
cymbals

CLICK!
claves

SLAPPED
slapstick

SILENTLY
triangle

DUCKS
recorder head (blow as hard as you can)

QUACKED
vibraslap

LAUGHED
slide whistle

Copyright © 2009 by HAL LEONARD CORPORATION
International Copyright Secured   All Rights Reserved
The original purchaser of this publication has permission to reproduce this page for educational use in one school only. Any other use is strictly prohibited.

OK TO REPRODUCE

DADDY FELL INTO THE POND

By Alfred Noyes (1880-1958)

Everyone **grumbled**. The sky was **gray**.

We had nothing to do and nothing to **say**.

We were nearing the end of a dismal **day**,

And then there seemed to be nothing beyond,

Then

Daddy fell into the pond!

And everyone's **face** grew **merry and bright**,

And **Timothy danced** for sheer delight.

"Give me the camera, **quick, oh quick!**

He's crawling out of the duckweed!" **Click!**

Then the gardener suddenly **slapped** his knee,

And doubled up, shaking **silently**,

And the **ducks** all **quacked** as if they were daft,

And it sounded as if the old drake **laughed**.

Oh, there wasn't a thing that didn't respond

When

Daddy fell into the pond!

Copyright © 2009 by HAL LEONARD CORPORATION
International Copyright Secured   All Rights Reserved
The original purchaser of this publication has permission to reproduce this poem for educational use in one school only. Any other use is strictly prohibited.

ELETELEPHONY

I am notorious for getting my words switched around when trying to explain things to my students. It is no wonder then, that I found this poem by Laura Richards so enticing. I easily understand how this delightful verse came to be.

Laura Elizabeth Richards was born in Boston, Massachusetts. Her parents were both well-known in their own professions. Her father, S.G. Howe, was a teacher, physician and abolitionist who co-founded the Perkins Institute for the Blind. This establishment is most noted for its work with students Anne Sullivan and Helen Keller. Laura's mother was the great poet, Julia Ward Howe, best known as the author of Battle Hymn of the Republic.

Laura Richards was successful, as well. Not only was she a Pulitzer Prize winning author and biographer, she was famous for her children's books and nonsense verse. In her prime she was often called the "Queen of Nonsense Verse."

Enjoy this poem and west bishes!

TEACHING SUGGESTIONS

1. Project the poem (found on CD-ROM) or hand out printed copies. Read the poem aloud for the students as they follow along, alternately patting a quarter note beat.

2. Discuss the strange words found in the poem and what combination of words was used to make the new vocabulary, i.e. "telephant" is a blend of tele-phone and ele-phant.

3. Repeat step #1 as the students speak the poem with you.

4. Finally, have the students read the poem aloud as they clap on the highlighted words. (To secure the feel for this meter even further, have students practice one more time reading the poem internally but continuing to clap on the highlighted words.)

5. Discuss the rhythm of the highlighted words (ti-ti ta) and write it on the board. Explain that each of the highlighted words will be performed to this rhythm.

6. Distribute instruments and have players practice on words as poem is recited.

"ELEPHANT ORFF MUSIC":

(If Orff instruments are not available, consider using keyboards, tone chimes or resonator bells.)

To Prepare: Isolate the bars on each instrument used for the given patterns; in addition, project the "Elephant Orff Music" or hand out printed copies.

1. Pat the BX crossover pattern while speaking the "think" words. Transfer to instruments and play. (Note: The "think" words used here will also help your students remember the names of the treble clef lines!)

2. Have students look at the visual of the AX/SX part. Together label the note names. Talk about the skips found in this ostinato and pretend to play this pattern in the air while speaking the "think" words. Transfer to instruments and play against the BX part.

3. Have the students look at the AG/SG ostinato and discuss the melodic direction for this pattern. Include a discussion of skips and steps. Once again, pretend to play this part in the air while speaking the "think" words. Then, transfer to instruments and play in ensemble with other instruments.

4. For presentation, layer in parts from bottom to top.

PRESENTATION SUGGESTION:

1. Choose a reader(s) to recite the poem as the instrumentalists play on their selected words.

2. For your presentation, perform the "Elephant Orff Music" as an intro, interlude between verses and coda.

ELETELEPHONY

ELEPHANT *conga drum*	**TELEPHANT** *wood block*	**ELEPHONE** *güiro*	**TELEPHONE** *triangle*
CERTAIN QUITE *tambourine*	**GOT IT RIGHT** *maracas*	**GOT HIS TRUNK** *hand drum*	**TELEPHUNK** *jingle bells*
GET IT FREE *cabasa* 	**TELEPHEE** *cymbals*	**DROP THE SONG** *claves*	**TELEPHONG** *cowbell* 

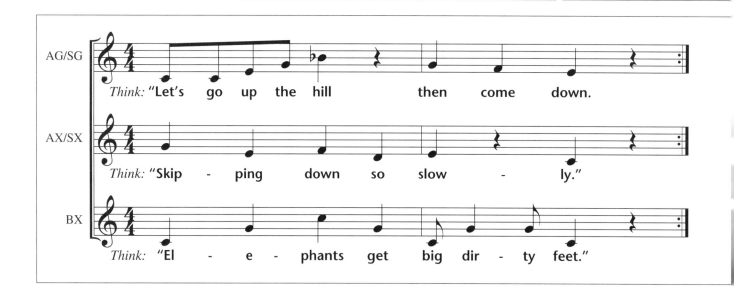

AG/SG — *Think:* "Let's go up the hill then come down.

AX/SX — *Think:* "Skip - ping down so slow - ly."

BX — *Think:* "El - e - phants get big dir - ty feet."

Copyright © 2010 by HAL LEONARD CORPORATION
International Copyright Secured   All Rights Reserved
The original purchaser of this publication has permission to reproduce this page for educational use in one school only. Any other use is strictly prohibited.

OK TO REPRODUCE

ELETELEPHONY

By Laura Richards

Once there was an **elephant**,

Who tried to use the **telephant**-

No! No! I mean an **elephone**

Who tried to use the **telephone**-

(Dear me! I am not **certain quite**

That even now I've **got it right**.)

Howe'er it was, he **got his trunk**

Entangled in the **telephunk;**

The more he tried to **get it free,**

The louder buzzed the **telephee**-

(I fear I'd better **drop the song**

Of elephop and **telephong!**)

OK TO REPRODUCE

Copyright © 2010 by HAL LEONARD CORPORATION
International Copyright Secured   All Rights Reserved
The original purchaser of this publication has permission to reproduce this poem for educational use in one school only. Any other use is strictly prohibited.

THE HARE AND THE TORTOISE

Aesop's Fables are a compilation of stories said to have been written by Aesop, a storyteller and slave who lived in ancient Greece in the fifth century B.C. The tales consist of animals that help to tell stories that teach a moral lesson.

Jean de La Fontaine was a French poet who lived in the seventeenth century. He was also a writer of fables, taking many of his inspirations from Aesop's Fables. This Sound Poem is an example of La Fontaine's work. He uses the story written by Aesop and creates a poem with the same theme.

If your students don't know this story, this poem should give them a delightful introduction. If they are familiar with this tale, they should find this version to be a great deal of musical fun. This is definitely one of those poems to act out and don't forget to spend time talking about the message found within the story.

TEACHING SUGGESTIONS:

1. Ask if any students are familiar with the Aesop's fable about the rabbit and the turtle having a race. Allow a student to share the story. If no one knows the tale, share the story either by rote or through a library resource.

2. Explain that the Sound Poem uses the story written by Aesop written as a poem.

3. Project the poem (found on CD-ROM) or hand out printed copies. Read the poem for the students as they follow along, emphasizing a 6/8 meter as you recite.

4. Define words that might be unfamiliar to the students, i.e. "quoth," "insane," "prescribe," "loafs," "frolicked" and "remarked."

5. Read the poem again while students look for the rhyming words throughout. Discuss where these are found.

6. Explain this poem is written in the style of a limerick with the first, second and fifth lines rhyming and the third and fourth lines rhyming.

7. Ask the class to read the poem with you as they clap on each special word.

8. Onc at a time, demonstrate how each instrument is played for these words as you then transfer students to the instruments.

9. When all instruments are placed, have students read the poem together, as instrumentalists play on their special word.

10. When the poem has been rehearsed with instruments, select several students to be narrators, one person to speak all of the "hare" lines and one for the "tortoise" part.

11. As suggested above, select students to act this one out. Many students can be added to this presentation by having them play the part of cheerleaders, trees, those holding the finish line tape, etc.

THE HARE AND THE TORTOISE

TORTOISE
conga drum

HARE
slide whistle

RUN
xylophone (or keyboard)

SPOT
triangle

BRAIN
hand drum

QUICK
slapstick

SUN
cymbals

WIN
tambourine

FROLICKED
vibraslap

DART
woodblock

SMART
finger cymbals

START
whistle (or recorder head)

OK TO REPRODUCE

Copyright © 2012 by HAL LEONARD CORPORATION
International Copyright Secured   All Rights Reserved
The original purchaser of this publication has permission to reproduce this page for educational use in one school only. Any other use is strictly prohibited.

THE HARE AND THE TORTOISE

By Jean de La Fontaine

Said the **Tortoise** one day to the **Hare**,
"I'll **run** you a race if you dare.
I'll bet you cannot
Arrive at that **spot**
As quickly as I can get there."

Quoth the **Hare**, "You are surely insane.
Pray, what has affected your **brain**?
You seem pretty sick,
Call a doctor in—**quick**,
And let him prescribe for your pain."

"Never mind," said the **Tortoise**. "Let's **run**!
Will you bet me?" "Why, certainly." "Done!"
While the slow **Tortoise** creeps,
Mr. **Hare** makes four leaps,
And then loafs around in the **sun**.

It seemed such a one-sided race,
To **win** was almost a disgrace.
So he **frolicked** about
Then at last he set out—
As the **Tortoise** was nearing the place.

Too late! Though he sped like a **dart**,
The **Tortoise** was first. She was **smart**;
"You can surely **run** fast,"
She remarked. "Yet you're last.
It is better to get a good start."

Copyright © 2012 by HAL LEONARD CORPORATION
International Copyright Secured All Rights Reserved
The original purchaser of this publication has permission to reproduce this poem for educational use in one school only. Any other use is strictly prohibited.

JOLLY OLD SAINT NICHOLAS

The holiday season brings many wonderful songs to hear and sing. Children particularly enjoy tunes about Santa Claus as they anticipate that special night called Christmas Eve. It seems they can never hear too many of these wonderful melodies.

Sometimes children don't realize that many of these holidays songs first started as poems. The focus behind our Sound Poem for this issue is a well-known Christmas tune that many of your students will know. Although "Jolly Old St. Nicholas" has been attributed to many individuals, no one actually knows who wrote the words or melody.

Your students will enjoy adding instruments to this familiar song as they learn it as a poem first and then sing it with added instruments to make for a delightful holiday experience.

TEACHING SUGGESTIONS:

1. Project the poem (found on CD-ROM) or hand out printed copies. Read the poem for the students as they follow along. Emphasize a 2/4 meter as you recite the rhyme.

2. Ask your students if they are familiar this poem and where they've heard it before. (Christmas song, "Jolly Old Saint Nicholas")

3. Have the students read along with you as they pat an alternating quarter note beat.

4. With students starting in a sitting position, ask them to read again as they stand up for each highlighted word found in the poem, and sit for the others.

5. Have students clap the rhythm for the "Jolly Old Saint Nicholas" motif as they speak the poem words. See if they can identify the rhythm syllables created from these words, and then have someone write this rhythm on a board. Transfer to jingle bells and have the student(s) practice.

6. Repeat the above procedure for the following motifs: "Christmas Eve," "stockings," "hanging," "shortest one."

7. For the remaining motifs, demonstrate how each instrument is played and transfer students to instruments one at a time.

8. When all instruments are placed, have students read the poem together as instrumentalists play on their special word(s).

9. When students are comfortable with this, repeat the above procedure while singing the song. (For an interesting twist, consider using a fast version of Pachelbel's "Canon in D Major" as an accompaniment.)

JOLLY OLD SAINT NICHOLAS

JOLLY OLD SAINT NICHOLAS
jingle bells

EAR
triangle

SOUL
maracas

SAY
claves

CHRISTMAS EVE
tambourine

MAN
conga drum

WHISPER
wind chimes (or bell tree)

CAN
vibraslap

CLOCK
woodblock

TWELVE
tone chimes (or resonator bells)

FAST
alto glockenspiel

DOWN
slide whistle

BROAD AND BLACK
cowbell

CREEP
güiro

STOCKINGS
hand drum

HANGING
alto xylophone (or keyboard)

SHORTEST ONE
finger cymbals

KNOW
cymbals

Copyright © 2011 by HAL LEONARD CORPORATION
International Copyright Secured   All Rights Reserved
The original purchaser of this publication has permission to reproduce this page for educational use in one school only. Any other use is strictly prohibited.

JOLLY OLD SAINT NICHOLAS

Traditional Carol

Jolly Old Saint Nicholas

Lean your **ear** this way.

Don't you tell a single **soul**

What I'm going to **say**.

Christmas Eve is coming soon,

Now, you dear old **man**.

Whisper what you'll bring to me.

Tell me if you **can**.

When the **clock** is striking **twelve**,

When I'm **fast** asleep,

Down the chimney **broad and black**

With your pack you'll **creep**.

All the **stockings** you will find

Hanging in a row.

Mine will be the **shortest one**,

You'll be sure to **know**.

Copyright © 2011 by HAL LEONARD CORPORATION
International Copyright Secured   All Rights Reserved
The original purchaser of this publication has permission to reproduce this poem for educational use in one school only. Any other use is strictly prohibited.

OK TO REPRODUCE

THE LAND OF NOD

With the winter months bringing us more time to stay indoors, what better way to spend that time than by taking a trip into "The Land of Nod"? The words of Robert Louis Stevenson once again provide us with a poem. Yet another selection from Stevenson's, A Child's Garden of Verses collection, will truly delight your students and, who knows, might even slow them down long enough to enjoy one of the Scottish writer's best poems.

TEACHING SUGGESTIONS:

1. Have the students lie on the floor (or put their heads down on their desks) and close their eyes. Turn down the lights in the room and read the poem to the class.

2. Ask them what the poet was referring to when he described "The Land of Nod." (sleeping and dreaming) Also, ask if this was a relaxing poem and why? Spend time talking about dreams and how fun they are to have, although sometimes quite strange.

3. Project the poem (found on CD-ROM) or hand out printed copies. Have the class read the poem along with you. Do not allow them to rush the tempo, but speak in a relaxed tone.

4. Teach the "sleep picture" icon by having students pat the BM/AM (BX/AX) pattern while speaking the suggested "think" words. Transfer to instruments and practice.

5. Repeat this procedure, asking them to alternately pat the AG/SG part while speaking the "think" words. Transfer to instruments and play against the BM/AM pattern.

6. Read through the poem again with the students as they snap once on each "special" word. (For "music," they should snap twice.) Have the instrumentalists play when they see the "sleep picture" icon.

7. Demonstrate how each instrument is played for the different motifs and transfer students to instruments one motif at a time.

8. When all instruments are placed, have the students read the poem together as instrumentalists play on their special word(s).

9. Finally, select four different readers to read one line of each verse. Add the instrumentalists and present.

For another presentation idea, consider playing the "sleep picture" music throughout the presentation instead as an accompaniment for the verses.

THE LAND OF NOD

SG/AG

Think: "Now I am a - sleep."

BM/AM
(or BX/AX)

Think: "Sleep, sleep, go to sleep."

DAY
finger cymbals

HOME
hand drum

NIGHT
vibraslap

NOD
woodblock

GO
xylophone

NONE
cymbals

STREAMS
tambourine

DREAMS
wind chimes

ME
slapstick

EAT
güiro

SIGHTS
triangle
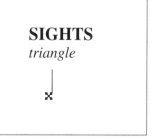

WAY
cowbell
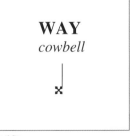

BACK
claves

CLEAR
maracas

MUSIC
resonator bells
(or tone chimes)

OK TO REPRODUCE

Copyright © 2011 by HAL LEONARD CORPORATION
International Copyright Secured   All Rights Reserved
The original purchaser of this publication has permission to reproduce this page for educational use in one school only. Any other use is strictly prohibited.

THE LAND OF NOD

By Robert Louis Stevenson

From breakfast on through all the **day**
At **home** among my friends I stay,
But every **night** I go abroad
Afar into the land of **Nod**.

The strangest things are there for **me**
Both things to **eat** and things to see,
And many frightening **sights** abroad
Till morning in the land of **Nod**.

All by myself I have to **go**,
With **none** to tell me what to do—
All alone beside the **streams**
And up the mountain-sides of **dreams**.

Try as I like to find the **way**,
I never can get **back** by day,
Nor can remember plain and **clear**
The curious **music** that I hear.

Copyright © 2011 by HAL LEONARD CORPORATION
International Copyright Secured   All Rights Reserved
The original purchaser of this publication has permission to reproduce this poem for educational use in one school only. Any other use is strictly prohibited.

LIMERICKS

A limerick is a light humorous five-line verse following the rhyming scheme of *aabba*. The name for this delightful poetic form is said to have started around 1895 from a county in the southwest republic of Ireland known as Limerick. Supposedly, it began as a party game in which each guest at a social gathering made up a verse using this rhyming couplet style. All those in attendance would respond by singing a refrain with the line, "Will you come up to Limerick?"

Edward Lear, an English artist, illustrator, author and poet is said to be the first to have penned poems in this manner. In 1846 he published *A Book of Nonsense*, a volume of limericks that went through three additions and helped to popularize this form. The limericks used in our *Sound Poem* collection are but a few found in this unique book.

Use this literature connection as a time for your students to write their own limericks. Offer them the opportunity to illustrate their verse and collate them into a book for your music library. Oh, and don't forget to add instruments to make this a unique and one-of-a-kind *Sound Poems* collection.

TEACHING SUGGESTIONS

Each of the suggested instruments should be played one time as the words of the poem are spoken, therefore the icons presented in this edition are represented as "word = instrument" icons.

1. Discuss limericks with your class. Give them information about the history, showing the location of Ireland on a map.

2. Read a limerick to your students (without them seeing it) and ask them to discover rhyming words.

3. Write the *aabba* rhyming scheme used in these poems on a board for the students to see.

4. Explain that Edward Lear is the poet for the limericks found in this edition. Project the poem (found on CD-ROM) or hand out printed copies. Have the students follow along as you read through the limericks. After reading each, have them recite the verse with you.

5. When the students are secure with the meter feel of this poetry, have them recite each again, clapping on the highlighted words.

6. Following limerick #1, transfer motifs one at a time to instruments. Use this same procedure for each of the following limericks.

7. Choose a reader for each limerick and perform with instruments.

8. For added fun, consider playing the rhythm of the limericks on drums (bongo, Conga, djembe, tubanos, etc.) as the verse is being recited. Continue to play the unpitched percussion on the highlighted words.

9. Try this idea once again while "thinking" the verses internally, still playing instruments.

LIMERICKS

LIMERICK #1

HILL *hand drum*	**STILL** *slapstick*	**UP** *alto xylophone*	**DOWN** *alto xylophone*	**GOWN** *cowbell*

LIMERICK #2

  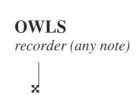   

BEARD *woodblock*	**FEARED** *vibraslap*	**OWLS** *recorder (any note)*	**HEN** *güiro*	**LARKS** *finger cymbals*	**WREN** *maracas*

LIMERICK #3

   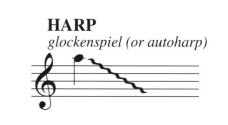

CHIN *tambourine*	**PIN** *triangle*	**SHARP** *keyboard*	**HARP** *glockenspiel (or autoharp)*

LIMERICK #4

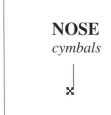   

NOSE *cymbals*	**TOES** *conga drum*	**LADY** *tone chimes (or resonator bells)*	**STEADY** *claves*

OK TO REPRODUCE

Copyright © 2010 by HAL LEONARD CORPORATION
International Copyright Secured   All Rights Reserved
The original purchaser of this publication has permission to reproduce this page for educational use in one school only. Any other use is strictly prohibited.

LIMERICKS

By Edward Lear

LIMERICK #1

There was an Old Man on a **hill**,
Who seldom, if ever, stood **still**;
He ran **up** and **down**,
In his Grandmother's **gown**,
Which adorned that Old Man on a **hill**.

LIMERICK #2

There was an Old Man with a **beard**,
Who said, "It is just as I **feared**!
Two **Owls** and a **Hen**,
Four **Larks** and a **Wren**,
Have all built their nests in my **beard**!"

LIMERICK #3

There was a Young Lady whose **chin**,
Resembled the point of a **pin**;
So she had it made **sharp**,
And purchased a **harp**,
And played several tunes with her **chin**.

LIMERICK #4

There was a Young Lady whose **nose**,
Was so long that it reached to her **toes**;
So she hired an Old **Lady**,
Whose conduct was **steady**,
To carry that wonderful **nose**.

Copyright © 2010 by HAL LEONARD CORPORATION
International Copyright Secured   All Rights Reserved
The original purchaser of this publication has permission to reproduce this poem for educational use in one school only. Any other use is strictly prohibited.

OK TO REPRODUCE

MARCHING SONG

Robert Louis Stevenson, a Scottish born and nationally known author, essayist and poet, best known for his adventurous novel, *Treasure Island*, brings to us this delightful and musical Sound Poem. The *Marching Song* is found in Stevenson's book of poems entitled *A Child's Garden of Verses and Underwoods* and is a great example of his unique playfulness he is able to portray through many of his writings.

There are numerous other charming poems found in this collection, including *Pirate Story, My Shadow, The Land of Nod* and *The Cow.* Consider having your students write their own Sound Poems from one of these short writings for a creative addition to this activity. I hope the contact your children make with this delightful writer will provide them with an interest in hearing and reading more of his works.

TEACHING SUGGESTIONS

To Prepare:

1. Project the poem (found on CD–ROM) or hand out printed copies. Read the poem aloud for the children as they follow along from the visual. (Recite the sonnet using simple meter.)

2. Define some of the words found in the poem, i.e. **cocks:** tips or tilts; **hearty:** excited, unrestrained; **Grenadier:** in the British army, a member of the first regiment of household infantry; **pillage:** loot, ransack.

3. Recite the poem again. As you read, ask students to march around the room, echoing back one line at a time as you play a steady beat on a drum.

4. Finally, have the students read the poem aloud as they clap on the highlighted words.

5. Although the rhythmic motifs are provided for you, consider challenging your students to discover the correct rhythm for each set of highlighted words. As these rhythms are discovered, write them on the board.

6. Clap the discovered rhythms using syllables, then with poem words. Transfer one motif at a time to instruments.

7. Choose a reader(s) to recite the poem as the instrumentalists play on their selected words.

8. For an extra challenge, try having your students recite the poem in compound meter, again playing their instruments at the appropriate time. Poll the class as to which setting (simple or compound) they like the best for this poem.

MARCHING SONG

COMB
güiro

MARCHING, HERE WE COME!
woodblock

WILLIE
cowbell

JOHNNIE BEATS THE DRUM
hand drum

MARY JANE
triangle

PETER LEADS THE REAR
tambourine

FEET
slapstick

EACH A GRENADIER
castanets

MARTIAL MANNER
claves

MARCHING DOUBLE-QUICK
temple block

NAPKIN
sandblocks

WAVES UPON THE STICK
cabasa

FAME
gong

PILLAGE
maracas

GREAT COMMANDER JANE
jingle bells

VILLAGE
finger cymbals

LET'S GO HOME AGAIN
conga drum

OK TO REPRODUCE

Copyright © 2010 by HAL LEONARD CORPORATION
International Copyright Secured   All Rights Reserved
The original purchaser of this publication has permission to reproduce this page for educational use in one school only. Any other use is strictly prohibited.

MARCHING SONG

By Robert Louis Stevenson

Bring the **comb** and play upon it!

Marching, here we come!

Willie cocks his highland bonnet,

Johnnie beats the drum.

Mary Jane commands the party,

Peter leads the rear;

Feet in time, alert and hearty,

Each a Grenadier!

All in the most **martial manner**

Marching double-quick;

While the **napkin**, like a banner,

Waves upon the stick!

Here's enough of **fame** and **pillage**,

Great commander Jane!

Now that we've been round the **village**,

Let's go home again.

Copyright © 2010 by HAL LEONARD CORPORATION
International Copyright Secured   All Rights Reserved
The original purchaser of this publication has permission to reproduce this poem for educational use in one school only. Any other use is strictly prohibited.

OK TO
REPRODUCE

MR. NOBODY

As a child, I can remember incidents happening in our home for which no one took the blame. It was as if there was an invisible person that caused the mischief to occur. Besides, it was a lot more fun to blame the mishaps on a magical character that always got away before we could make him take responsibility for his actions!

Thus is the theme behind the poem "Mr. Nobody." Your students will surely want to share stories of their own of how this sly fellow causes trouble in their home. And what makes this poem even more unique is the author. Since no one seems to take credit for its origination, it must have been written by … you guessed it … Mr. Nobody!

TEACHING SUGGESTIONS:

1. Project the poem (found on CD-ROM) or hand out printed copies. Read the poem aloud as the students follow along.

2. Discuss the mischief behind Mr. Nobody. Explain that the word "prithee" means pray thee.

3. Read again, having the students join along with you as they clap on each special word.

4. Point out the "Mr. Nobody" motif. Together clap the pattern while speaking rhythm syllables.

5. Repeat this process, but have the students speak the "think" words while clapping. Finally, have them practice clapping while "thinking" these words.

6. Explain that this pattern is performed each time after "Mr. Nobody" is spoken in the poem.

7. Transfer a student(s) to the instrument(s) and practice.

8. Demonstrate how each of the other instruments is played for their special word(s) and transfer students to instruments one at a time.

9. When all instruments are placed, select a narrator(s) to read the poem as instrumentalists play on their special word(s).

10. For added fun, choose someone to be "Mr. Nobody" and act this poem out.

11. For an extended activity, considering writing other things "Mr. Nobody" has done to cause trouble. Work with the students to write another verse for the poem. Add instruments and enjoy!

MR. NOBODY

MAN
hand drum

MOUSE
triangle

HOUSE
vibraslap

FACE
cymbals

CRACKED
slapstick

MR. NOBODY
conga drum

Think: No-bod-y,   No-bod-y,   Mis - ter   No-bod-y.

TEARS
finger cymbals

LEAVES
maracas

PULLS
xylophone

SCATTERS
bell tree (wind chime)

SQUEAKING
recorder head

OILING
slide whistle

DOOR
woodblock

BLINDS
güiro

INK
claves

SEE
triangle

OK TO REPRODUCE

Copyright © 2011 by HAL LEONARD CORPORATION
International Copyright Secured   All Rights Reserved
The original purchaser of this publication has permission to reproduce this page for educational use in one school only. Any other use is strictly prohibited.

MR. NOBODY

Anonymous

I know a funny little **man**,
As quiet as a **mouse**,
Who does the mischief that is done
In everybody's **house**!
There's no one ever sees his **face**,
And yet we all agree
That every plate we break was **cracked**
By **Mr. Nobody**.

'Tis he who always **tears** our books,
Who **leaves** the door ajar,
He **pulls** the buttons from our shirts,
And **scatters** pins afar;
That **squeaking** door will always squeak,
For prithee, don't you see,
We leave the **oiling** to be done
By **Mr. Nobody**.

The finger marks upon the **door**
By none of us are made;
We never leave the **blinds** unclosed
to let the curtains fade;
The **ink** we never spill; the boots
That lying around you **see**
Are not our boots; they all belong
To **Mr. Nobody**!

MR. NOBODY
conga drum

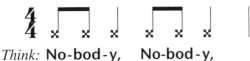
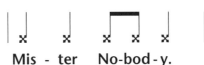

Think: **No-bod-y, No-bod-y, Mis - ter No-bod-y.**

Copyright © 2011 by HAL LEONARD CORPORATION
International Copyright Secured   All Rights Reserved
The original purchaser of this publication has permission to reproduce this poem for educational use in one school only. Any other use is strictly prohibited.

THE PREAMBLE

The Preamble to the Constitution, established by our Founding Fathers, is a powerful introductory statement to the document that has shaped our country. It provides a summary of what the authors felt the Constitution meant and what they hoped it would achieve. Although this statement is not a poem, its message reads poetically and is an important declaration that all Americans should know by memory.

Even though the celebration of Constitution Day only happens once a year on September 17th, I hope you find this idea of teaching the Preamble through music to be a source that helps your students lock in the high ideals of our forefathers as they carry the message with them throughout their lives. After all, we ARE the People.

TEACHING SUGGESTIONS

1. Ask students about their knowledge of the Preamble. Explain the purpose of this document, why it was written and what it introduces.

2. Read the Preamble to your class in free form and discuss the definitions of words found there, i.e. "union," "justice," "domestic tranquility," etc.

3. Project the Preamble (found on CD-ROM) or hand out printed copies. Have students follow as you recite the rhythmic document. Challenge them to perform the following body percussion ostinato as the document is read:

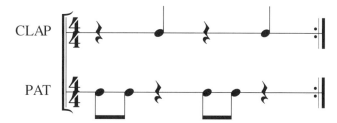

4. Ask students to echo speak this document in two-measure phrases. Continue until learned. (Once learned, challenge your older students to rhythm speak/clap the entire selection.)

5. Point out the special words found and clap the rhythm of each one.

6. Have children read through the document, clapping on the special words.

7. Transfer specials words to these suggested instruments. (Be careful to add only a few instruments at a time.)

"We, the People of the United States". . . . . . all instruments

"perfect Union". . . . . triangle

"Justice" . . . . C bourdun on bass xylophone or C on bass bar

"domestic Tranquility". . . . wood block

"common defense" . . . . tambourine

"general Welfare". . . . . claves

"Liberty". . . . . güiro

"Posterity". . . . . temple blocks (high to low)

"ordain and establish" . . . . hand drum

"Constitution". . . . . Conga drum

"United States of America". . . . . all instruments

8. Finally, perform the Preamble with instruments, while those not playing perform the body percussion ostinato as all speak together.

9. As an extension, consider internalizing the document as all instruments and body percussion continue to perform.

THE PREAMBLE

Setting by Cristi Cary Miller

We, the Peo-ple of the U - nit - ed States, in Or-der to form a more
per - fect Un - ion, es - tab-lish Jus - tice, in-sure do-mes-tic Tran - quil - i - ty, pro - vide for the com-mon de - fense, pro - mote the gen - er - al Wel - fare, and se - cure the Bless-ings of Li - ber - ty to our - selves and our Pos - ter - i - ty, do or - dain and es - tab - lish this Con - sti - tu - tion for the U - nit - ed States of A - mer - i - ca.

OK TO REPRODUCE

Copyright © 2009 by HAL LEONARD CORPORATION
International Copyright Secured   All Rights Reserved
The original purchaser of this publication has permission to reproduce this poem for educational use in one school only. Any other use is strictly prohibited.

SANTA'S NEW IDEA

Ok, I'll admit it. I still believe in Santa Claus. Yes, I still believe on Christmas Eve that jolly old elf plops down my chimney, eats my cookie (unless I ate it before he got there), drinks my milk and leaves behind my chosen gifts. Perhaps that's why this poem intrigued me so. I never considered that these gifts might have chosen to live with *me* instead!

Although the author for this verse is unknown, he or she must still believe in Santa Claus, also. How else could this person have created such a delightful illustration of how toys make their way to the homes of girls and boys during this special holiday? I hope you enjoy this new twist to a familiar story.

TEACHING SUGGESTIONS:

1. Project the poem (found on CD-ROM) or hand out printed copies. Read the poem aloud as the students follow along while patting a quarter note beat.

2. Repeat procedure, having them read along with you.

3. Ask students to identify the highlighted words in the poem. For fun, have them make up a motion for each "special" word(s).

4. Now, challenge the students to read the poem again as they perform their created actions at the appropriate places.

5. Demonstrate how each instrument is played on its iconic word and transfer students to instruments one at a time.

6. When all instruments are placed, practice the poem as all read aloud with actions and instrumentalists play on their words.

7. For fun, try reading the poem again internally as instrumentalists continue to play and other perform movement.

SANTA'S NEW IDEA

SANTA CLAUS
jingle bells

Think: "San - ta   Claus"

GIFTS
cowbell

CHRISTMAS DAY
triangle

Think: "Christ - mas   Day"

TOYS
woodblock

GIRLS AND BOYS
alto xylophone (or keyboard)

Think: "girls and boys"

CLEAR
finger cymbals

SPEEDING
alto xylophone (or keyboard)

JOY AND CHEER
tambourine

Think: "joy   and   cheer"

FAR AND NEAR
hand drum

Think: "far   and   near"

IDEA
vibraslap

HOMES
tone chimes (or resonator bells)

SNOW
bell tree (or wind chime)

TOTS
slide whistle

HURRAH! HURRAH!
maracas

Think: "Hur - rah!   Hur - rah!"

PLAY
claves

CAREFULLY
cabasa (or sandblocks)

Think: "care - ful - ly"

SOCKS
cymbals

TREE
conga drum

YOU
slapstick

OK TO REPRODUCE

Copyright © 2010 by HAL LEONARD CORPORATION
International Copyright Secured   All Rights Reserved
The original purchaser of this publication has permission to reproduce this page for educational use in one school only. Any other use is strictly prohibited.

SANTA'S NEW IDEA

Author Unknown

Said **Santa Claus** one winter's night,
"I really think it's only right
That **gifts** should have a little say
'Bout where they'll be on **Christmas Day**."

So then and there he called the **toys**,
Intended for good **girls and boys**,
And when they'd settled down to hear,
He made his plan for them quite **clear**.

These were his words:

Soon now, said he,
You'll all be **speeding** off with me
To bring the Christmas **joy and cheer**
To little ones both **far and near**.

Here's my **idea**, it seems but fair
That you should each one have a share
In choosing **homes** where you will stay
On and after **Christmas Day**.

Now the next weeks before we go
Over the miles of glistening **snow,**
Find out the **tots** that you like best
And think much nicer than the rest.

The **toys** called out, "**Hurrah! Hurrah!**
What fun to live always and **play**
With folks we choose – they'll surely be
Selected very **carefully**."

So, children dear, when you do see
Your **toys** in **socks** or on a **tree**,
You'll know in all the world 'twas **you**
They wanted to be given to.

Copyright © 2010 by HAL LEONARD CORPORATION
International Copyright Secured   All Rights Reserved
The original purchaser of this publication has permission to reproduce this poem for educational use in one school only. Any other use is strictly prohibited.

SOME ONE

Here is a poem that is sure to ignite the creative thoughts in your young learners. It was written by Walter John de la Mare, an English poet, short story writer and novelist. He is probably best remembered for his works for children entitled "The Listeners." De la Mare's first book, *Songs of Childhood*, was published under the name Walter Ramal. Strangely enough, in addition to his writings for children, he was also a significant writer of ghost stories.

Our selection is found in a book of poetry entitled *Peacock Pie, a Book of Rhymes*. If your students enjoy this choice, they would most certainly like the others found in this collection. But for now, this one's sure to "knock" their socks off!

TEACHING SUGGESTIONS:

1. Teach the following body percussion ostinato to the students:

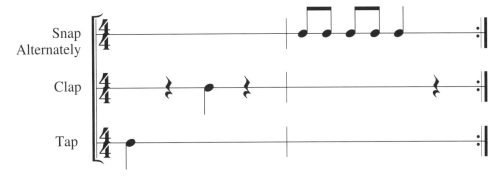

2. When they are secure with this pattern, have them perform this ostinato as you recite the poem.

3. Discuss with your students the meaning of the word "nought." (This word is an alternative spelling for the word "naught" which means "nothing.")

4. Because there might be a variety of ways to speak the rhythm of this poem, ask the students to echo you in two-line intervals in order to learn the rhythm you've selected.

5. Project the poem (found on CD-ROM) or hand out printed copies. Then ask students to read the entire poem together as they clap (or pat) on the highlighted words.

6. Demonstrate the rhythm of each motif and how each instrument is played for the special words. Transfer students to instruments one word at a time.

7. When all instruments are placed, select a narrator(s) to read the poem as instrumentalists play on their special word(s).

8. In conclusion, select a small group of children to perform the above ostinato, substituting the following instruments for the indicated body percussion:
   pat = güiro, clap = drum, snaps = rhythm sticks

SOME ONE

KNOCKING
woodblock

WEE, SMALL DOOR
rhythm sticks

SURE-SURE-SURE
tambourine

LISTENED
glockenspiel

OPENED
cowbell

LEFT AND RIGHT
temple blocks
(or piccolo blocks)

A-STIRRING
xylophone (or maracas)

STILL DARK NIGHT
triangle

BEETLE
finger cymbals

TAP-TAPPING
claves

SCREECH OWL'S CALL
recorder head

WHISTLING
slide whistle
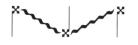

FALL
xylophone

ALL
hand drum

OK TO REPRODUCE

Copyright © 2011 by HAL LEONARD CORPORATION
International Copyright Secured   All Rights Reserved
The original purchaser of this publication has permission to reproduce this page for educational use in one school only. Any other use is strictly prohibited.

SOME ONE

By Walter de la Mare

Some one came **knocking**

At my **wee, small door**;

Some one came **knocking**,

I'm **sure-sure-sure**;

I **listened**, I **opened**,

I looked to **left and right**,

But nought there was **a-stirring**

In the **still dark night**,

Only the busy **beetle**

Tap-tapping in the wall.

Only from the forest

The **screech owl's call**.

Only the cricket **whistling**

While the dewdrops **fall**,

So I know not who came **knocking**,

At **all**, at **all**, at **all**.

Copyright © 2011 by HAL LEONARD CORPORATION
International Copyright Secured   All Rights Reserved
The original purchaser of this publication has permission to reproduce this poem for educational use in one school only. Any other use is strictly prohibited.

THE SPIDER AND THE FLY

For as long as I can remember, I have enjoyed the poem "The Spider and the Fly." It does a wonderful job of creating the imagery of the cunning spider as she approaches the fly about being her "guest." Although not in totality, this partial representation of the poem is sure to "crawl" its way into the hearts of your students.

Mary Howitt was an English poet and author. She penned this ode in 1829 and it instantly caught the attention of many. Today it has been made a parody by such great writers as Lewis Carroll in his *Alice's Adventures Underground* as well as in the cartoon series, *Teenage Mutant Ninja Turtles*.

TEACHING SUGGESTIONS

1. Project the poem (found on CD-ROM) or hand out printed copies. Read the poem aloud as the students follow along. After each verse, have them recite the Spider Melody *think* words, i.e. "creep-y, crawl-y," etc. (found at bottom of sound effects). As they speak, have them alternately pat the beat.

2. Now, read the poem together, having students clap one time for each "special" word.

3. Point out the different characters found in the selection (Spider and Fly) and indicate which lines each speaks. Then, divide the class into two groups, spiders and flies, and have those groups read their appropriate lines of the poem while they continue to clap the "special" words. Switch parts and perform again.

4. To teach the Spider Melody, ask the students to again practice speaking the *think* words for this part while patting. Transfer the pats to the BX.

5. Discuss how the keyboard notes in the melody are chromatic and allow the students to watch as you play this melodic line. Transfer a student to the keyboard and have him/her play against the BX part.

6. For the remaining motifs, demonstrate how each instrument is played on its iconic word and transfer students to instruments one at a time.

7. Select a reader(s) for each character of the poem. Encourage the narrators to use dramatic voices as they recite their parts.

8. Add instruments and have the Spider Melody play between verses and at the conclusion for a "creepy" presentation.

THE SPIDER AND THE FLY

PARLOUR
woodblock

SPIDER
güiro

FLY
glockenspiel

WINDING STAIR
slide whistle

DOWN
alto xylophone

BED
hand drum

TUCK YOU IN
cowbell

PANTRY
claves

SLICE
maracas (or cabasa)

WEB
tambourine

ROBES
finger cymbals

CREST(ED)
cymbals

EYES
triangle

BUZZING
vibraslap

JUMPED
conga drum

SPIDER MELODY

Keyboard

Think: "Creep-y, crawl-y, creep-y, crawl-y, creep-y, crawl-y, STOP!"

BX

Copyright © 2010 by HAL LEONARD CORPORATION
International Copyright Secured   All Rights Reserved
The original purchaser of this publication has permission to reproduce this page for educational use in one school only. Any other use is strictly prohibited.

THE SPIDER AND THE FLY

By Mary Howitt

Will you walk into my **parlour**?

said the **spider** to the **fly**.

'Tis the prettiest little **parlour**

that ever you did spy,

The way into my **parlour**

is up a **winding stair**,

And I've a many curious things to

show when you are there.

Oh no, no, said the little **Fly**,

to ask me is in vain,

For who goes up your **winding stair**,

can ne'er come **down** again.

(chant Spider Melody)

I'm sure you must be weary, dear,

with soaring up so high.

Will you rest upon my little **bed**?

said the **Spider** to the **Fly**.

There are pretty curtains drawn around;

the sheets are fine and thin,

And if you like to rest awhile,

I'll snugly **tuck you in**!

Oh no, no, said the little **Fly**,

for I've often heard it said

They never, never wake again,

who sleep upon your **bed**!

(chant Spider Melody)

Said the cunning **Spider** to the **Fly**,

Dear friend what can I do,

To prove the warm affection

I've always felt for you?

I have within my **pantry**,

good store of all that's nice.

I'm sure you're very welcome;

will you please to take a **slice**?

Oh no, no, said the little **Fly**,

Kind Sir, that cannot be,

I've heard what's in your **pantry**,

and I do not wish to see!

(chant Spider Melody)

Copyright © 2010 by HAL LEONARD CORPORATION
International Copyright Secured   All Rights Reserved
The original purchaser of this publication has permission to reproduce this poem for educational use in one school only. Any other use is strictly prohibited.

The **Spider** turned him round about,

and went into his den,

For well he knew the silly **Fly**

would soon come back again.

So he wove a subtle **web**,

in a little corner sly,

And set his table ready,

to dine upon the **Fly**.

Then he came out to his door again,

and merrily did sing,

Come hither, hither, pretty **Fly**,

with the pearl and silver wing,

Your **robes** are green and purple,

there's a **crest** upon your head,

Your **eyes** are like the diamond bright,

but mine are dull as lead!

(chant Spider Melody)

Alas, alas! How very soon

this silly little **Fly**,

Hearing his wily, flattering words,

came slowly flitting by

With **buzzing** wings she hung aloft,

then near and nearer drew,

Thinking only of her brilliant **eyes**,

and green and purple hue,

Thinking only of her **crested** head,

poor foolish thing! At last,

Up **jumped** the cunning **Spider**,

and fiercely held her fast.

He dragged her up his **winding stair**,

into his dismal den,

Within his little **parlour**,

but she ne'er came out again!

(chant Spider Melody)

And now dear little children,

who may this story read,

To idle, silly flattering words,

I pray you ne'er give heed.

Unto an evil counselor,

close heart and ear and eye,

And take a lesson from this tale,

of the **Spider** and the **Fly**.

(chant Spider Melody)

OK TO REPRODUCE

Copyright © 2010 by HAL LEONARD CORPORATION
International Copyright Secured   All Rights Reserved
The original purchaser of this publication has permission to reproduce this poem for educational use in one school only. Any other use is strictly prohibited.

ST. PATRICK WAS A GENTLEMAN

I've always loved St. Patrick's Day. I like wearing green on this day, not wanting to stand the chance of being pinched for failure to wear this traditional color. Many places in my city provide customary Irish folk music for easy listening and, occasionally, I get to eat some green eggs. Mostly, though, I enjoy the fact that St. Patrick's Day seems to signify the beginning of spring.

The origin of this holiday dates back to AD 385 with the birth of a boy in Scotland. At the age of 14 or so, he was captured and taken to Ireland as a slave. There he devoted himself to God and, upon his release, turned to missionary work, preaching throughout Ireland. Through his ministry, he converted many native pagans to Christianity. He is even said to have given a sermon on a hillside that drove all the snakes from Ireland, although today we know that no snakes were ever native to this country. Patrick died on March 17 AD 461, which has become the officially holiday now known as St. Patrick's Day. The St. Patrick's Day custom came to America in 1737, where it was first celebrated in the town of Boston.

This Sound Poem comes from a traditional Irish song. The lyrics originally consisted of three stanzas written by Henry Bennett and a Mr. Toleken of Cork, in 1814. Although there are additional verses that can be found, this is the most common. May the luck of the Irish be yours today!

TEACHING SUGGESTIONS:

1. Ask the students what they know about St. Patrick's Day and the traditions and symbols that surround this celebration. (*Wear green, shamrock, parades, originated in Ireland, etc.*) Share with them some background on this popular holiday. Also, show them where Ireland is located on a world map.

2. Project the poem (found on CD-ROM) or hand out printed copies. Read the poem for the students as they follow along. Emphasize a 6/8 meter as you recite the rhyme. Note: Although the rhythm endings for this poem are left up

to the interpretation of the reader, consider using this rhythm in order for students to play the phrase endings successfully on their instruments, i.e.

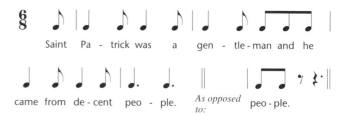

3. Have the students read along with you as they alternately pat a quarter/eighth note pattern. (For your younger learners, have them echo speak one line at a time to help with words and rhythms.)

4. Remove the visual of the poem and see if they can remember things about St. Patrick by ASKING: What kind of man was St. Patrick? (*a gentleman*); Where did he build his church? (*Dublin*); What was his father? (*a Gallagher*); What was his mother? (a Brady); What was his aunt? (*an O'Shaughnessy pronounced Oh-SHAW-neh-see*), etc.

5. Display the poem again and point out how the answers for your questions came from the special words.

6. One at a time, demonstrate how each instrument is played for the rhythm of these words. Then transfer students to the instruments.

7. 7. When all instruments are placed, have students read the poem together as instrumentalists play on their special word.

8. 8. For added fun, have a group of students make a standing circle and ask them to gallop sideways CW for the first phrase of the poem, switching CCW for the second, etc. as it is performed.

YouTube provides many listening examples of this Irish song. Always preview videos before showing in the classroom.

ST. PATRICK WAS A GENTLEMAN

GENTLEMAN
hand drum

PEOPLE
tambourine

CHURCH
tone chimes (or resonator bells)

STEEPLE
woodblock

GALLAGHER
xylophone (or keyboard)

BRADY
finger cymbals

O'SHAUGNESSY
claves

GRADY
sandblocks

FIST
slapstick

CLEVER
triangle

SNAKES
maracas

TOADS
güiro

FOREVER
conga drum

Copyright © 2012 by HAL LEONARD CORPORATION
International Copyright Secured   All Rights Reserved
The original purchaser of this publication has permission to reproduce this page for educational use in one school only. Any other use is strictly prohibited.

OK TO REPRODUCE

ST. PATRICK WAS A GENTLEMAN

By Henry Bennett

Saint Patrick was a **gentleman**,

and he came from decent **people**,

In Dublin town he built a **church**,

and on it put a **steeple**;

His father was a **Gallagher**,

his mother was a **Brady**,

His aunt was an **O'Shaughnessy**,

and his uncle was a **Grady**.

Then success to bold Saint Patrick's **fist**,

He was a saint so **clever**,

He gave the **snakes** and **toads** a twist,

and banished them **forever**!

Copyright © 2012 by HAL LEONARD CORPORATION
International Copyright Secured   All Rights Reserved
The original purchaser of this publication has permission to reproduce this poem for educational use in one school only. Any other use is strictly prohibited.

THE STORY OF FIDGETY PHILIP

Heinrich Hoffman, the author of this *Sound Poem*, was a German psychiatrist who lived from 1809 to 1894. One Christmas he wanted to buy a picture book for his son. Not liking what he found in the stores, he decided to purchase a notebook to write his own stories with pictures to give as his gift. A publisher friend read the collection and a year later, in 1845, persuaded him to print these tales. Soon after, this book was called *Struwwelpeter* and became popular with children throughout Europe. The original title, "Funny stories and droll pictures," shows that entertainment was part of Hoffman's intentions. Perhaps you've known a few "Fidgety Phils" in your lifetime. If so, you will be as entertained as your students with this story.

TEACHING SUGGESTIONS:

1. Project the poem (found on CD-ROM) or hand out printed copies. Read the poem aloud as the students follow along.

2. Discuss words that may be unfamiliar to the students, i.e. "bade," "grave," "cross," "fret."

3. Read the poem again, having the students join along with you as they clap once on each special word.

4. For fun, have the students reverse the process by "thinking" the poem silently but clapping/speaking the special words out loud. (Hint: For your young readers, consider pointing to the words as they follow along reading silently.)

5. Demonstrate how each instrument is played for their special word and transfer students to instruments one at a time.

6. When all instruments are placed, select a narrator(s) to read the poem as instrumentalists play on their special word(s).

7. Here's another poem that would be fun to act out. (*I'm sure you'll be able to find the right student in your class to play the part of Fidgety Phil!*)

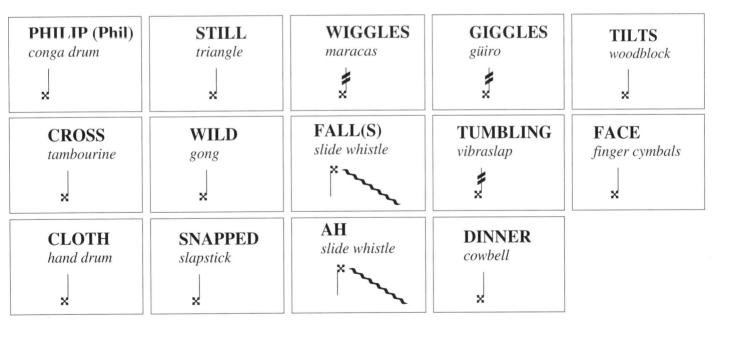

PHILIP (Phil) *conga drum*	STILL *triangle*	WIGGLES *maracas*	GIGGLES *güiro*	TILTS *woodblock*
CROSS *tambourine*	WILD *gong*	FALL(S) *slide whistle*	TUMBLING *vibraslap*	FACE *finger cymbals*
CLOTH *hand drum*	SNAPPED *slapstick*	AH *slide whistle*	DINNER *cowbell*	

OK TO REPRODUCE

Copyright © 2011 by HAL LEONARD CORPORATION
International Copyright Secured   All Rights Reserved
The original purchaser of this publication has permission to reproduce this page for educational use in one school only. Any other use is strictly prohibited.

THE STORY OF FIDGETY PHILIP

By Heinrich Hoffman

"Let me see if **Philip** can
Be a little gentleman;
Let me see if he is able
To sit **still** for once at table."
Thus Papa bade **Phil** behave;
And Mamma looked very grave.
But fidgety **Phil**,
He won't sit still;
He **wiggles**,
And **giggles**,
And then, I declare,
Swings backwards and forwards,
And **tilts** up his chair,
Just like any rocking-horse-
"**Philip**! I am getting **cross**!"

See the naughty, restless child
Growing still more rude and **wild**,
Till his chair **falls** over quite.
Philip screams with all his might,
Catches at the cloth, but then
That makes matters worse again.
Down upon the ground they **fall**,
Glasses, plates, knives, forks, and all.
How Mamma did fret and frown,
When she saw them **tumbling** down!
And Papa made such a **face**!
Philip is in sad disgrace.

Where is **Philip**, where is he?
Fairly covered up you see!
Cloth and all are lying on him;
He has pulled down all upon him.
What a terrible to-do!
Dishes, glasses, **snapped** in two!
Here a knife, and there a fork!
Philip, this is cruel work.
Table all so bare, and **ah**!
Poor Papa, and poor Mamma
Look quite **cross**, and wonder how
They shall have their **dinner** now.

OK TO REPRODUCE

Copyright © 2011 by HAL LEONARD CORPORATION
International Copyright Secured   All Rights Reserved
The original purchaser of this publication has permission to reproduce this poem for educational use in one school only. Any other use is strictly prohibited.

'TWAS THE NIGHT BEFORE CHRISTMAS

What would December be without a reading of Clement Clarke Moore's famous poem, "'Twas the Night Before Christmas"? This celebrated work was first published anonymously in 1823 in a New York newspaper and was entitled "A Visit from St. Nicholas." It is largely responsible for the origination of Santa Claus concerning his appearance, mode of transportation and names of his reindeer. Today this delightful piece is often read aloud to children on Christmas Eve as they await the arrival of the joyous little man in the furry red suit.

Adding instruments to this poem will certainly bring musical fun to your students. I hope this seasonal offering becomes a permanent part of your classroom holiday season presentation. "Happy Christmas to all and to all a good-night!"

TEACHING SUGGESTIONS

1. Project the poem (found on CD-ROM) or hand out printed copies. Read the poem aloud for the students as they follow along. Read again as the students say the poem with you.

2. Introduce each motif as it happens in the poem. For the melodic motifs ("Too" and "Jelly"), follow this procedure:

   a. Clap the rhythm speaking rhythm syllables.

   b. Discuss pitch direction and sing with solfege in rhythm.

   c. Sing again using *think* words.

   d. Transfer to suggested instruments.

   For rhythmic motifs ("There" and "Reindeer"), follow this procedure:

   a. Clap the rhythm while speaking the rhythm syllables.

   b. Clap again using the *think* words.

   c. Transfer to suggested instruments.

3. For all other motifs, demonstrate sounds on the suggested instruments as students follow visuals. Transfer instruments to students.

4. The last line of the poem does not have a motif, but should be spoken all together as a group. Practice saying the last line of the poem together, working towards expressive speaking.

5. Explain that each motif happens after the designated motif word (or at the end of each four-line stanza.)

6. Choose a reader(s) to recite the poem as the instrumentalists play after their designated stanza.

7. Consider acting out the poem for a visual effect.

'TWAS THE NIGHT BEFORE CHRISTMAS

THERE
jingle bells

Think: "Jin - gle bells,   jin - gle bells"

NAP
snoring sound

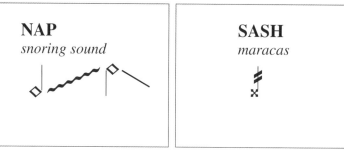

SASH
maracas

REINDEER
woodblock   *slapstick*

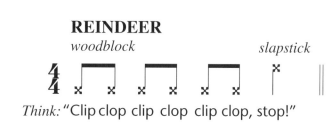

Think: "Clip clop clip clop clip clop, stop!"

NAME
whistling sound

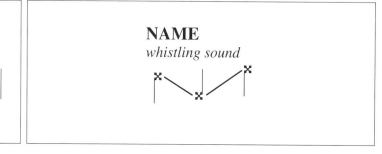

ALL
glockenspiel

TOO
keyboard (or singing voices)

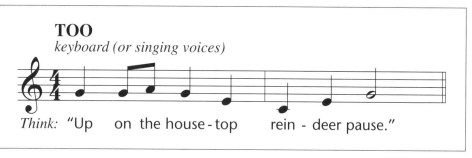

Think: "Up   on the house - top   rein - deer pause."

BOUND
slide   conga
whistle   drum

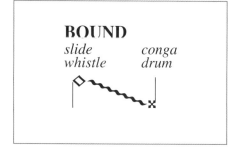

PACK
tambourine

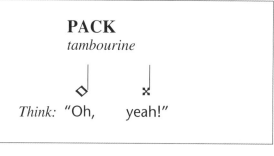

Think: "Oh,   yeah!"

SNOW
bell tree

JELLY
alto xylophone

Think: "Ho! Ho! Ho! Ho! Ho!"

DREAD
vibraslap

ROSE
slide   triangle
whistle

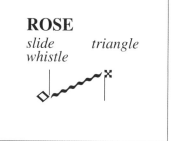

OK TO REPRODUCE

Copyright © 2009 by HAL LEONARD CORPORATION
International Copyright Secured   All Rights Reserved
The original purchaser of this publication has permission to reproduce this page for educational use in one school only. Any other use is strictly prohibited.

'TWAS THE NIGHT BEFORE CHRISTMAS

By Clement Clark Moore

'Twas the night before Christmas, when all through the house
Not a creature was stirring, not even a mouse;
The stockings were hung by the chimney with care,
In hopes that St. Nicholas soon would be **there**.

The children were nestled all snug in their beds,
While visions of sugar plums danced in their heads;
And mamma in her 'kerchief, and I in my cap,
Had just settled down for a long winter's **nap**.

When out on the lawn there arose such a clatter,
I sprang from the bed to see what was the matter.
Away to the window I flew like a flash,
Tore open the shutters and threw up the **sash**.

The moon on the breast of the new-fallen snow
Gave the luster of mid-day to objects below,
When, what to my wondering eyes should appear,
But a miniature sleigh, and eight tiny **reindeer**,

With a little old driver, so lively and quick,
I knew in a moment it must be St. Nick.
More rapid than eagles his coursers they came,
And he whistled, and shouted, and called them by **name**;

"Now, Dasher! Now, Dancer! Now, Prancer and Vixen!
On, Comet! On, Cupid! On, Donder and Blitzen!
To the top of the porch! To the top of the wall!
Now dash away! Dash away! Dash away **all**!"

As dry leaves that before the wild hurricane fly,
When they meet with an obstacle, mount to the sky,
So up to the housetop the coursers they flew,
With the sleigh full of toys, and St. Nicholas, **too**.

Copyright © 2009 by HAL LEONARD CORPORATION
International Copyright Secured   All Rights Reserved
The original purchaser of this publication has permission to reproduce this poem for educational use in one school only. Any other use is strictly prohibited.

OK TO REPRODUCE

'TWAS THE NIGHT BEFORE CHRISTMAS CONTINUED

And then, in a twinkling, I heard on the roof
The prancing and pawing of each little hoof.
As I drew in my hand, and was turning around,
Down the chimney St. Nicholas came with a **bound**.

He was dressed all in fur, from his head to his foot,
And his clothes were all tarnished with ashes and soot;
A bundle of toys he had flung on his back,
And he looked like a peddler just opening his **pack**.

His eyes — how they twinkled! His dimples — how merry!
His cheeks were like roses, his nose like a cherry!
His droll little mouth was drawn up like a bow,
And the beard of his chin was as white as the **snow**;

The stump of a pipe he held tight in his teeth,
And the smoke it encircled his head like a wreath;
He had a broad face and a little round belly,
That shook, when he laughed like a bowlful of **jelly**.

He was chubby and plump, a right jolly old elf,
And I laughed when I saw him, in spite of myself;
A wink of his eye and a twist of his head,
Soon gave me to know I had nothing to **dread**.

He spoke not a word, but went straight to his work,
And filled all the stockings; then turned with a jerk,
And laying his finger aside of his nose,
And giving a nod, up the chimney he **rose**.

He sprang to his sleigh, to his team gave a whistle,
And away they all flew like the down of a thistle.
But I heard him exclaim, as he drove out of sight,
"Happy Christmas to all, and to all a good night."

Copyright © 2009 by HAL LEONARD CORPORATION
International Copyright Secured   All Rights Reserved
The original purchaser of this publication has permission to reproduce this poem for educational use in one school only. Any other use is strictly prohibited.

TWO LITTLE KITTENS

The winter weather gives us good reasons to stay inside. No one wants to be caught in the ice and snow when there's a nice warm alternative found by a fireplace! Such is the case for the two fuzzy characters in this Sound Poem.

Although the writer of this rhyme is unknown, this poem can be found in many children's poetry collections. Perhaps it is because this whimsical account of two kittens reminds children that friendships are important. It also might remind them that sometimes quarreling can take them to places they'd rather not be! Enjoy this furry tale!

TEACHING SUGGESTIONS:

1. Project the poem (found on CD-ROM) or hand out printed copies. Read the poem aloud using a 6/8 meter feel as the students follow along.

2. Read the verse again, using a 4/4 meter feel. Let the students decide which one they like the best.

3. Once the rhythm has been selected, have the students read through the poem with you, clapping once for each special word.

4. Demonstrate how each instrument is played for its special word(s) and transfer students to instruments one at a time.

5. When all instruments are placed, select a narrator(s) to read the poem as instrumentalists play on their special word(s).

6. This is a good one to act out, so choose characters to play the two kittens, the mouse and the old woman.

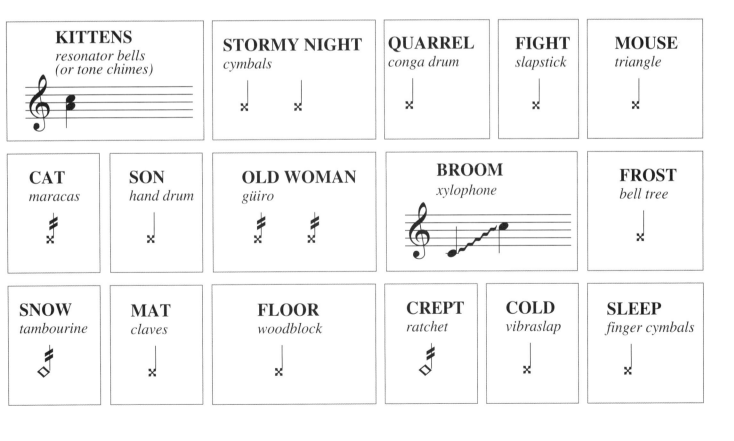

OK TO REPRODUCE

Copyright © 2010 by HAL LEONARD CORPORATION
International Copyright Secured   All Rights Reserved
The original purchaser of this publication has permission to reproduce this page for educational use in one school only. Any other use is strictly prohibited.

TWO LITTLE KITTENS

Anonymous

Two little **kittens**, one **stormy night**,
Began to **quarrel**, and then to **fight**;
One had a **mouse**, the other had none,
And that's the way the **quarrel** begun.

"I'll have that **mouse**," said the biggest **cat**;
"You'll have that **mouse**? We'll see about that!"
"I will have that **mouse**," said the eldest **son**.
"You shan't have the **mouse**," said the little one.

I told you before 'twas a **stormy night**
When these two little **kittens** began to **fight**;
The **old woman** seized her sweeping **broom**,
And swept the two **kittens** right out of the room.

The ground was covered with **frost** and **snow**,
And the two little **kittens** had nowhere to go;
So they laid them down on the **mat** at the door,
While the **old woman** finished sweeping the **floor**.

Then they **crept** in, as quiet as mice,
All wet with the **snow**, and **cold** as ice,
For they found it was better, that **stormy night**,
To lie down and **sleep** than to **quarrel** and **fight**.

OK TO REPRODUCE

Copyright © 2010 by HAL LEONARD CORPORATION
International Copyright Secured   All Rights Reserved
The original purchaser of this publication has permission to reproduce this poem for educational use in one school only. Any other use is strictly prohibited.

THE UNSEEN PLAYMATE

The great poet, Carl Sandburg, once said, "Poetry is a packsack of invisible keepsakes." He surely understood the delight behind putting imagination to paper through prose. Robert Louis Stevenson is the author of this Sound Poem. Stevenson was a Scottish novelist and poet. His best-known books include *Treasure Island, Kidnapped* and *Strange Case of Dr. Jekyll and Mr. Hyde.* As a child, he was frequently ill and spent many days in bed. He wasn't able to attend a regular school because of his illness. Yet he was a gifted storyteller and wrote many books including one book of poems entitled *A Child's Garden of Verses.* It is from this book that we get our poem.

Enjoy this classic with your students as they grow to appreciate one of the world's greatest storytellers.

TEACHING SUGGESTIONS:

1. Project the poem (found on CD-ROM) or hand out printed copies. Read the poem for the students as they follow along. Emphasize the 6/8 meter as you recite the verses.

2. Discuss with your students why this playmate is "unseen." (*He's imaginary.*) See if any of them have had an imaginary friend.

3. Spend time talking about some of the words found in the poem which might be unfamiliar to the students:
   abroad = *about; away from home*
   laurels = *small European evergreen trees*
   inhabits = *to live or dwell in*
   bids = *to command*

4. Have the students read the poem with you as they pat a steady beat.

5. Ask them to read again as they clap (or pat) on the highlighted words.

6. Demonstrate how each instrument is played for their special word and transfer students to instruments one at a time.

7. When all instruments are placed, select a narrator(s) to read the poem as instrumentalists play on their special word(s).

8. For fun, give each student a paper and pencil and have them draw what they think the "unseen playmate" looks like. Allow students time to share these pictures with their classmates.

THE UNSEEN PLAYMATE

PLAYMATE
güiro

HAPPY
triangle

LONELY
rhythm sticks

GOOD
resonator bells (or tone chimes)

HEARD
recorder head (or whistle)

SAW
maracas (or cabasa)

ABROAD
xylophone (or keyboard)

HOME
hand drum

LAURELS
woodblock

GRASS
vibraslap

SINGS
slide whistle

LITTLE
finger cymbals

BIG
conga drum

TIN
cowbell

BED
bell tree (or wind chime)

SLEEP
glockenspiel

CUPBOARD
claves

SHELF
slapstick

OK TO REPRODUCE

Copyright © 2011 by HAL LEONARD CORPORATION
International Copyright Secured   All Rights Reserved
The original purchaser of this publication has permission to reproduce this page for educational use in one school only. Any other use is strictly prohibited.

THE UNSEEN PLAYMATE

By Robert Louis Stevenson

When children are playing alone on the green,
In comes the **playmate** that never was seen.
When children are **happy** and **lonely** and **good**,
The Friend of the Children comes out of the wood.

Nobody **heard** him and nobody **saw**,
His is a picture you never could draw,
But he's sure to be present, **abroad** or at **home**,
When children are **happy** and playing alone.

He lies in the **laurels**, he runs on the **grass**,
He **sings** when you tinkle the musical glass;
Whene'er you are **happy** and cannot tell why,
The Friend of the Children is sure to be by!

He loves to be **little**, he hates to be **big**,
'Tis he that inhabits the caves that you dig;
'Tis he when you play with your soldiers of **tin**
That sides with the Frenchman and never can win.

'Tis he, when at night you go off to your **bed**,
Bids you go to **sleep** and not trouble your head;
For wherever they're lying, in **cupboard** or **shelf**,
'Tis he will take care of your playthings himself!

OK TO REPRODUCE

Copyright © 2011 by HAL LEONARD CORPORATION
International Copyright Secured All Rights Reserved
The original purchaser of this publication has permission to reproduce this poem for educational use in one school only. Any other use is strictly prohibited.

YOU ARE OLD, FATHER WILLIAM

This poem was written by the famous author, Charles Lutwidge Dodgson. You've never heard of him, you say? That's because in his writings he used a surname. Perhaps you know him better by the pseudonym, Lewis Carroll. Not only did this English author pen the following delightful poem, but he's responsible for great works such as *Alice's Adventures in Wonderland*, along with its sequel, *Through the Looking-Glass*. In addition, he also wrote the well known poem "Jabberwocky." Some interesting information about Dodgson is that he was identified at a young age at being quite intelligent yet he suffered from a stammer, also known as a stutter. Amazingly, this speech difficulty did not stop him from singing in front of audiences, who found him quite good. Sometimes music makes the difference.

I hope you enjoy this amusing poem!

TEACHING SUGGESTIONS

1. Project the poem (found on CD-ROM) or hand out printed copies. Read the poem for the students as they follow along. Emphasize the 6/8 meter as you recite the verses.

2. Spend time talking about some of the words found in the poem which might be unfamiliar to the students:

    incessantly = ceaseless; unending

    sage = a profoundly wise person

    supple = limber

    shilling = a former monetary unit of the United Kingdom, the 20th part of a pound

    suet = the hard, fatty tissue about the loins and kidneys of beef, sheep, etc.; used in cooking and for making tallow

    airs = assumed haughtiness

3. Have the students read the poem with you as they pat a steady beat.

4. Ask them to read again as they clap (or pat) on the highlighted words.

5. When students are secure with the rhythm of the poem, isolate the two reoccurring patterns found throughout ("You are old," and "In my youth,"). Clap the patterns for the students while speaking the think words. Have them echo speak the patterns and then transfer to instruments.

6. Ask the students to recite the poem again incorporating the new instruments.

7. Repeat step #5 for the motif "again and again."

8. For the remaining motifs, demonstrate how each instrument is played, transferring students to instruments one at a time.

9. Choose one reader for each verse and ask them to speak expressively as the instrumentalists play on their selected words.

10. For fun, act this one out!

YOU ARE OLD, FATHER WILLIAM

YOU ARE OLD
conga drum

Think: "You are old,"

HAIR
finger cymbals

AGE
cowbell

IN MY YOUTH
triangle

Think: "In my youth"

BRAIN
tambourine

AGAIN AND AGAIN
woodblocks

Think: "a - gain and a - gain"

FAT
cymbals

BACK SOMERSAULT
slide whistle

LIMBS
glockenspiel (resonator bells or keyboard)
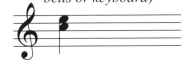

BOX
slapstick

JAWS
vibraslap

GOOSE
güiro

WIFE
maracas (or cabasa)

LIFE
hand drum

EYE
claves

NOSE
whistle (or recorder head)

AIRS
wind chimes (or bell tree)

DOWNSTAIRS
xylophone (or keyboard)

OK TO REPRODUCE

Copyright © 2009 by HAL LEONARD CORPORATION
International Copyright Secured   All Rights Reserved
The original purchaser of this publication has permission to reproduce this page for educational use in one school only. Any other use is strictly prohibited.

YOU ARE OLD, FATHER WILLIAM

By Lewis Carroll

"**You are old**, Father William," the young man said,
"And your **hair** has become very white;
And yet you incessantly stand on your head.
Do you think, at your **age**, it is right?"

"**In my youth**," Father William replied to his son,
"I feared it might injure the **brain**;
But, now that I'm perfectly sure I have none,
Why, I do it **again and again**."

"**You are old**," said the youth, "As I mentioned before,
And have grown most uncommonly **fat**;
Yet you turned a **back somersault** in at the door.
Pray, what is the reason of that?"

"**In my youth**," said the sage, as he shook his grey locks,
"I kept all my **limbs** very supple
By the use of this ointment-one shilling the **box**.
Allow me to sell you a couple?"

"**You are old**," said the youth, "And your **jaws** are too weak
For anything tougher than suet;
Yet you finished the **goose**, with the bones and the beak.
Pray, how did you manage to do it?"

"**In my youth**," said the father, "I took to the law,
And argued each case with my **wife**;
And the muscular strength, which it gave to my jaw,
Has lasted the rest of my **life**."

"**You are old**," said the youth, "one would hardly suppose
That your **eye** was steady as ever;
Yet, you balanced an eel on the end of your **nose**.
What made you so awfully clever?"

"I have answered three questions, and that is enough,"
Said his father. "Don't give yourself **airs**!
Do you think I can listen all day to such stuff?
Be off, or I'll kick you **downstairs**!"

Copyright © 2010 by HAL LEONARD CORPORATION
International Copyright Secured   All Rights Reserved
The original purchaser of this publication has permission to reproduce this poem for educational use in one school only. Any other use is strictly prohibited.